To my deux unbelievable enfants, Casey and Jake—J.S.

To my planet Corona amikos: Rory, Steve-o, Mark-o and the Beck—L.S.

BALONEY

(HENRY P.)

received and decoded by Jon Scieszka

visual recreation by Lane Smith

GRAFICA MOLLY LEACH

VIKING

Last Tuesday morning, at 8:37 a.m.,
Henry P. Baloney was finally late for class once too often.

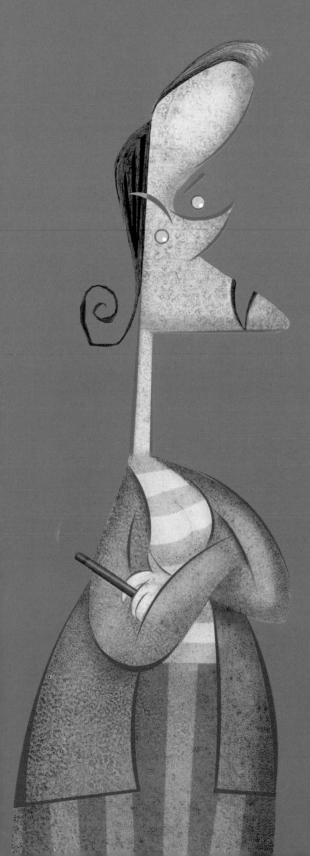

"That's it," said Miss Bugscuffle. "Permanent Lifelong Detention ... unless you have one very good and very believable excuse."

"Well I would have been exactly on time," said Henry.

"But ...

I MISPLACED MY TRUSTY ZIMULIS.

THEN I ... UM ... FOUND IT ON MY DESKI.

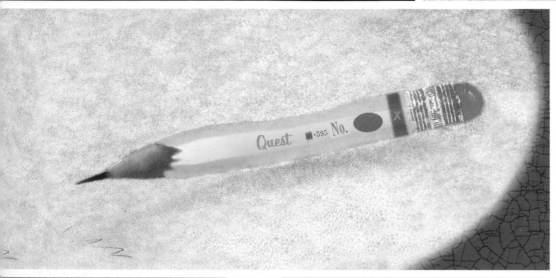

BUT...

SOMEONE HAD PUT MY DESKI IN A *TORAKKU*.

THE TORAKKU DROVE ME RIGHT HERE TO *SZKOLA*. BUT...

THEN IT DROVE RIGHT PAST.

I GRABBED MY ZIMULIS AND JUMPED OUT.

BUT . . .

I JUMPED

SMACK IN THE

MIDDLE OF A...

RAZZO LAUNCH PAD.

ESCAPE
ESCAPE

CHEESCAPE

I USED MY ZIMULIS TO POP OPEN THE ESCAPE PORDO. BUT...

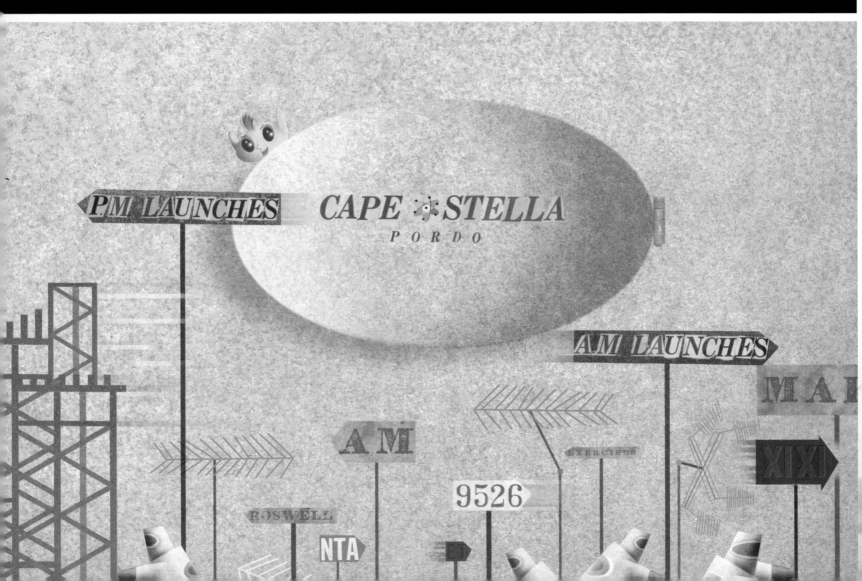

P.M LAUNCHES

CAPE ☀ STELLA
PORDO

AM LAUNCHES

MAR

AM

EXERCISES

XIX

ROSWELL

9526

NTA

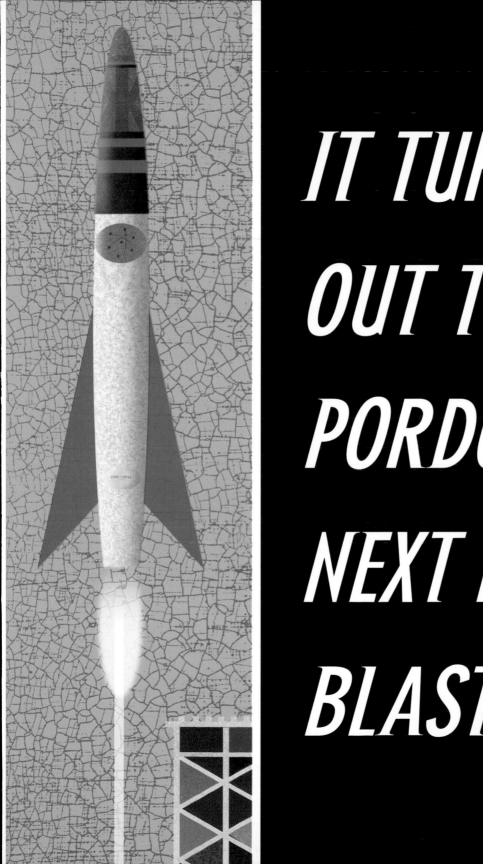

IT TURNED OUT TO BE A PORDO INTO THE NEXT RAZZO BLASTING OFF.

I JAMMED THE RAZZO CONTROLS WITH MY ZIMULIS SO I COULD LAND BEHIND SZKOLA AND STILL BE ON TIME. BUT...

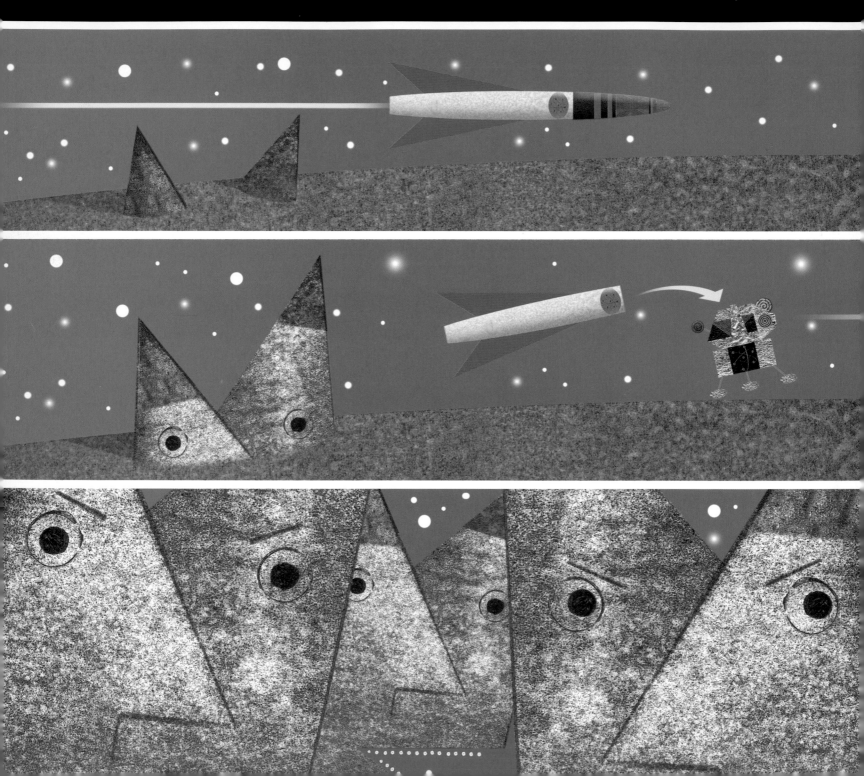

I ENTERTAINED THE ASTRO GUYS WITH MY VERY FUNNY *PIKSAS. BUT...*

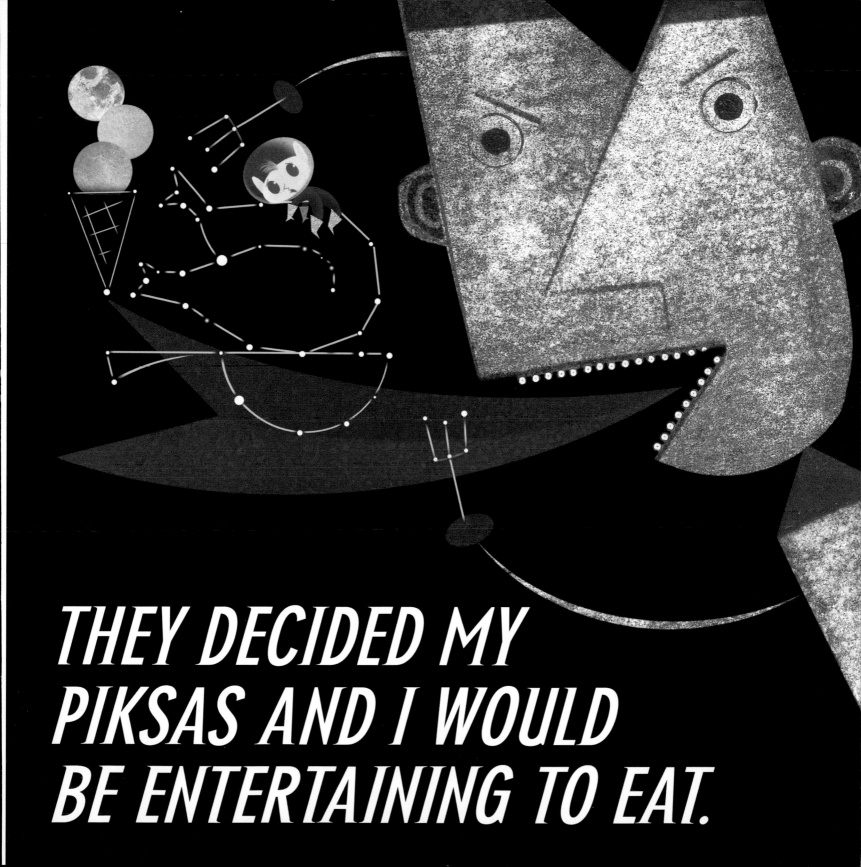

THEY DECIDED MY PIKSAS AND I WOULD BE ENTERTAINING TO EAT.

I CHANGED THEIR MINDS WITH GIADRAMS AND CUCALATIONS SO FANTASTIC THEY...

CROWNED ME KUNINGAS OF THE WHOLE PLANET.

AND ACCIDENTALLY USED THE WORD FOR "DOOFBRAIN."

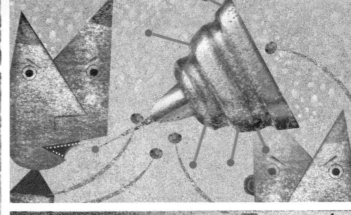

THEIR *BLASSA* WITH MY *ZIMULIS*.

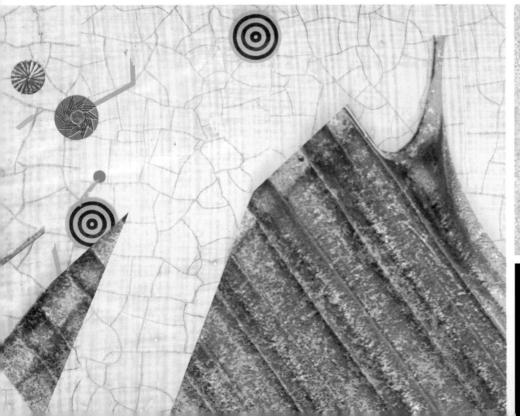

BUT...

THEY MADE A NEW PLAN TO SEND ME BACK IN A SIGHING FLOSSER ...

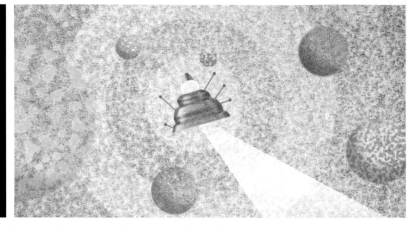

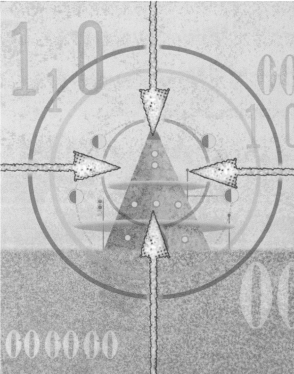

TO FRACASSE OUR SZKOLA.

I ERASED THE SIGHING FLOSSER FRACASSE INSTRUCTIONS. BUT...

I ALSO ERASED THE SIGHING FLOSSER PORDO LOCK AND FELL OUT.

I DROPPED

LIKE AN

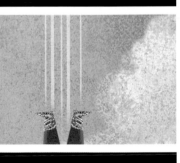

UYARAK.

I WAS ONLY THREE SECONDS AWAY FROM ZERPLATZEN ALL OVER THE SPEELPLAATS. NOT EVEN MY TRUSTY ZIMULIS COULD SAVE ME."

"So what did you do?" said Miss Bugscuffle. "How could you possibly save yourself?"

"I suddenly remembered . . .

THAT FALLING BODIES OBEY THE LAW OF GRAVITY.

AND I HAVEN'T LEARNED THE LAW OF GRAVITY YET. SO I STOPPED AND CAME TO SZKOLA.

All of which
made me
exactly seven
minutes late
this aamu."

"Henry P. Baloney,"
said Miss Bugscuffle.
"That is unbelievable.
But today's assign-
ment is to compose a
tall tale. So why don't
you sit down and get
started writing."

"I'd love to,"
said Henry.
"But ...

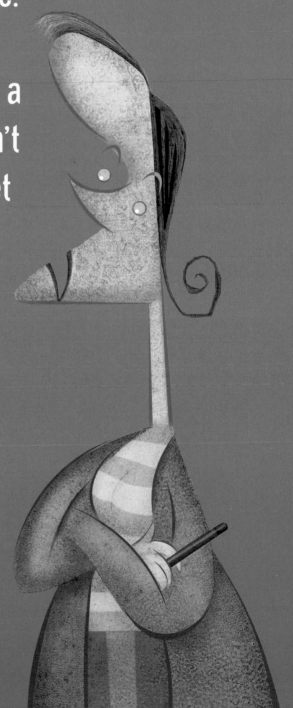

I SEEM TO HAVE MISPLACED MY ZIMULIS."

AFTERWORD

This transmission was received directly from deep space. Once the signals were decoded, it became clear that this was a story about a lifeform similar to many Earthlings. Even more amazing was the discovery that the story is written in a combination of many different Earth languages including Latvian, Swahili, Finnish, Esperanto, and Inuktitut.

Who knows why.

DECODER

AAMU (Finnish) morning

ASTROSUS (Latin) unlucky

BLASSA (Uqbaric) raygun

BUTTUNA (Maltese) button

CUCALATIONS (Transposition) calculations

DESKI (Swahili) desk

FRACASSE (French) shatter

GIADRAMS (Transposition) diagrams

KUNINGAS (Estonian) king

PIKSA (Melanesian Pidgin) picture

PORDO (Esperanto) door

RAZZO (Italian) rocket

SIGHING FLOSSER (Spoonerism) flying saucer

SPEELPLAATS (Dutch) playground

SZKOLA (Polish) school

TORAKKU (Japanese) truck

TWRF (Welsh) noise

UYARAK (Inuktitut) stone

ZERPLATZEN (German) splattering

ZIMULIS (Latvian) pencil

© 2001

VIKING
Published by the Penguin Group
Penguin Books Ltd, 27 Wrights Lane, London W8 5TZ, England
Penguin Putnam Inc., 375 Hudson Street, New York, New York 10014, USA
Penguin Books Australia Ltd, Ringwood, Victoria, Australia
Penguin Books Canada Ltd, 10 Alcorn Avenue, Toronto, Ontario, Canada M4V 3B2
Penguin Books India (P) Ltd, 11 Community Centre, Panchsheel Park, New Delhi — 110 017, India
Penguin Books (NZ) Ltd, Cnr Rosedale and Airborne Roads, Albany, Auckland, New Zealand
Penguin Books (South Africa) (Pty) Ltd, 5 Watkins Street, Denver Ext 4, Johannesburg 2094, South Africa

On the World Wide Web at: www.penguin.com

Penguin Books Ltd, Registered Offices: Harmondsworth, Middlesex, England

First published 2001
1 3 5 7 9 10 8 6 4 2

Set in Global
Printed in Hong Kong

British Library Cataloguing in Publication Data
A CIP catalogue record for this book is available from the British Library

ISBN 0-670-91143-7

DESIGN: Molly Leach, New York, New York